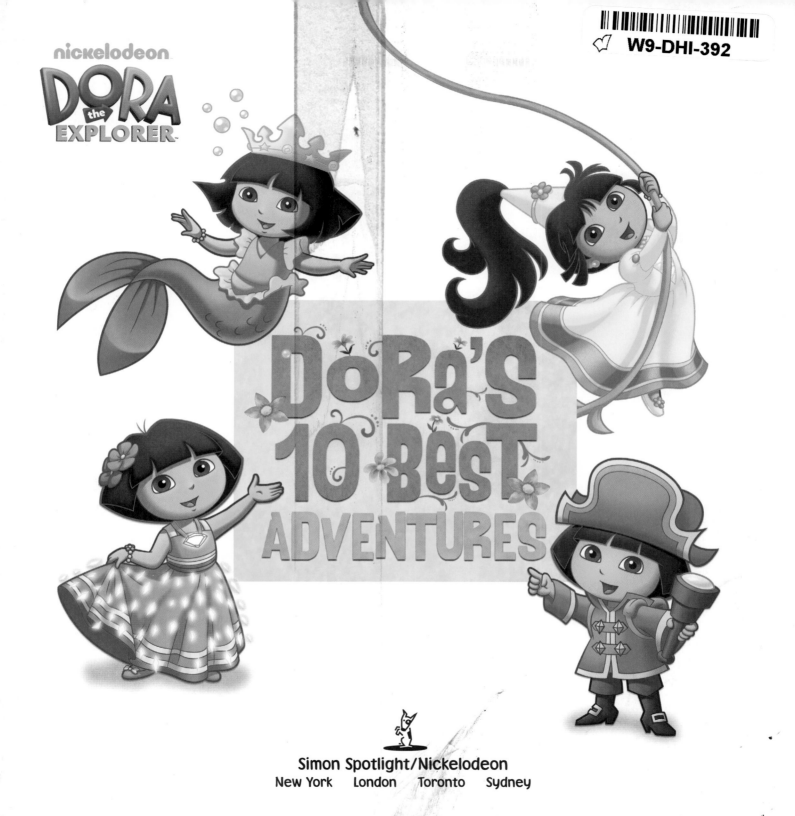

nickelodeon

DORA the EXPLORER

DORA'S 10 BEST ADVENTURES

Simon Spotlight/Nickelodeon
New York   London   Toronto   Sydney

ConTenTs

Dora's Backpack

adapted by Sarah Willson
based on the teleplay by Eric Weiner
illustrated by Robert Roper

¡Hola! I'm Dora, and this is my friend Backpack! I need to return eight books to the library, and Backpack's going to help me. We have to get there before it closes. Will you help us too?

Great! First we need to find Boots the monkey. Do you see him?

Now we have to find the quickest way to the library. Who do we ask for help when we don't know which way to go? Map! There's a map inside my Backpack. Say "Map!"

Map says we have to go over the Troll Bridge and then cross Turtle River. That's how we'll get to the Library.

We made it to the Troll Bridge, but the Grumpy Old Troll won't let us cross unless we solve his riddle. Can you help us solve it?

"Here is one of my hardest quizzers," says the Grumpy
Old Troll. "To cut through the net, use a pair of . . ."
What do you think the answer is?

Scissors! That's right. Can you find a pair of scissors in my Backpack? We need them to cut through the net.

We did it! We made it over the Troll Bridge. So next comes Turtle River, but there's a storm cloud! It's going to rain!

Can you see if Backpack has something to keep us dry?

You found the umbrella!
Oh, no! That storm cloud made the ground
all wet. Now Boots is stuck in the Icky-Sticky Sand.

Let's check Backpack for something to help Boots. Can you find it?

Right, a rope! I need your help to pull Boots out. Use your hands and pull, pull, pull! Great job!

Now we need to take that boat across Turtle River. Before we get into the boat what should we wear to be safe? Check Backpack!

Right! Life jackets! Uh-oh. I hear Swiper the fox. He's trying to swipe them! If you see him, say "Swiper, no swiping!"

Thanks for helping us stop Swiper. Now we can cross Turtle River. We're almost at the Library. Can you see it?

Here we are at the Library.

Oh, no! The door is closed, but we can use Spanish to open it. If you say *"abre,"* the door will open. Can you say *"abre"*?

We did it! Now we can return my library books on time.

Can you count to make sure Val the librarian has all eight books from Backpack?

Hooray for Backpack! We couldn't have done it without her or you! Thanks for helping!

30

adapted by Alison Inches
based on the teleplay by Chris Gifford
illustrated by A&J Studios

¡Hola! I'm Dora, and this is my best friend, Boots. Today I got a present from my grandma. *Mi abuela* made me a necklace to match my bracelet. I really love it! Do you like presents too?

Uh-oh, that sounds like Swiper the fox! That sneaky fox will try to swipe my necklace. If you see Swiper, say "Swiper, no . . ."

Oh, no! We're too late. Swiper swiped my necklace and threw it to the top of Star Mountain. I really love my necklace. Will you help Boots and me get it back? Great!

Star Mountain is where the Explorer Stars live. If we call them, they will help us find my necklace. To call the Explorer Stars, we have to say *"Estrellas."* Say it with us. *"¡Estrellas!"*

Look! The Explorer Stars came! There's Tool Star, the Explorer Star with lots of tools. And there is Saltador, the super jumping Explorer Star. And there is Glowy, the bright light Explorer Star. The Explorer Stars will help us get my necklace back.

First we have to figure out how to get to the top of Star Mountain. Who do we ask for help when we don't know which way to go? Map! Say "Map!"

Map says that to get my necklace back, we have to run up fifteen steps. Then we have to climb all the way up the Diamond. And that's how we'll get to the Giant Star on top of Star Mountain.

39

Do you see the steps? *¿Dónde están?* There they are! But they're covered in fog! We need Tool Star to help us through the fog. Which tool can Tool Star use to get us through the fog? *¡Sí!* A fan!

Tool Star is fanning the fog out of the way. Good fanning!

We made it through the fog to the steps. Count the fifteen steps with me. *Uno, dos, tres, cuatro, cinco, seis, siete, ocho, nueve, diez, once, doce, trece, catorce, quince.*

Great counting! We made it up all fifteen steps. But look at all this bubbling green goo! It's blocking our way! We need an Explorer Star to help us get past this goo. Glowy, the bright light Star, can help us melt the goo with her hot lights. Go, Glowy!

Yay! We made it past the goo! So where do we go next? Yeah, the Diamond! Wait, I hear a rumbling sound. It's a giant rock!

Look! It's Saltador, the super jumping Explorer Star. Saltador can help us jump over the falling rock. Let's jump on the count of three. Count with me. *¡Uno, dos, TRES!* We jumped over the giant rock! *¡Gracias, Saltador!*

45

Now let's use these star handles to climb the Diamond. The stars are red and green, *roja y verde*. We have to follow the pattern to climb to the top. Will you help? Say *"¡Roja! ¡Verde! ¡Roja! ¡Verde!"* Good job!

We made it up the Diamond! Thanks for helping. Now we need to go to the Giant Star to get my necklace back. *¿Dónde está?*

There's the Giant Star! And there's my necklace! To get up the Giant Star, we're going to need a long rope. Will you check Backpack for a long rope? You have to say "Backpack!"

Do you see a long rope? *¡Muy bien!* Very good! Thanks!

Now I have to throw the rope to the top of the Giant Star. Wish me luck! Say *"¡Buena suerte!"*
Wow, I did it! Thanks for your help!

Now I have to grab the rope and climb to the top. Will you help me climb? Say "¡Sube! ¡Sube, sube, sube!" Great climbing! Do you see my necklace?

I see it! My necklace! My necklace!

¡Lo hicimos! We did it! You helped me get back my necklace, and the Explorer Stars helped too. *¡Gracias, estrellas!*

I couldn't have done it without you. *¡Gracias!* Thanks for helping!

Dora Saves MERMAID KINGDOM!

adapted by Michael Teitelbaum
based on the teleplay by Valerie Walsh
illustrated by Artful Doodlers

¡Hola! I'm Dora, and this is my best friend, Boots. We love the beach. We love the ocean, the warm sand, the bright blue sky, and the sunny sun.

Today is Clean-Up-the-Beach Day! That's when we make sure the beach is nice and clean!

Let's pick up all the garbage and put it in the garbage bag. Do you see any garbage on the beach? *¡Sí!* There's a juice box! And there's a food wrapper!

¿Qué más? What else do you see? If you see more garbage, say "¡Basura!"

¡Mira! There is a big clam on the beach. To tell the big clam to open, say "*¡Abre!*"

Great job! This big clam has
a special story to tell us.

61

The clam's story is about the Mermaid Kingdom.

Once upon a time a mean octopus dumped garbage all over the Mermaid Kingdom. Luckily, a mermaid named Mariana found a magic crown so she could wish all the garbage away. But a wave washed away Mariana's magic crown, and now she can't stop the mean octopus!

We need to help Mariana and the Mermaid Kingdom by finding that magic crown. Where could it be?

If you see the crown, say *"¡Corona!"* Do you see the magic crown? There it is!

Now we can bring the crown back to Mariana! Let's find the Mermaid Kingdom! Who do we ask for help when we don't know which way to go?

¡Sí! Map! Say "Map!"

Map says that we have to cross the Seashell Bridge and then go through Pirate Island to get to the Silly Sea. That's where we will find the Mermaid Kingdom. Come on! *¡Vámonos!*

We made it to the Seashell Bridge, but we can't get across! That mean octopus has covered the bridge with garbage. Let's look inside Backpack for something to clean up the bridge. Say "Backpack!"

Is there anything in Backpack that we can use to clean up the bridge?

¡Si! A vacuum cleaner!

Now that we cleaned Seashell Bridge, we can get across. Let's count the shells as we cross. *Uno, dos, tres, cuatro, cinco, seis.* One, two, three, four, five, six.

¡Gracias! Thanks for helping us cross the bridge.

We made it to Pirate Island, but the Coconut Trees are in our way.

The Pirate Piggies show us how to do the Coconut Conga to get past the trees. Ready? Wiggle, wiggle, wiggle!

Now we need to cross the Silly Sea. Look at all these Silly Sea animals. Who can help us swim past them all and through the Silly Sea? Yeah, dolphins!

My cousin Diego can help us call the dolphins.
To help Diego call the dolphins, we need to say "Squeak, squeak!"

We made it to the Mermaid Kingdom! Let's give Mariana back her magic crown so she can clean up the Mermaid Kingdom.

Oh, no! We're too late! The octopus threw a big net over Mariana. Now she's trapped!

Ooooh! Mariana gave me the crown just in time! I put it on, and now I'm a mermaid! *¡Fantástico!*

The magic crown lets me have one wish. What should we wish for?

Let's wish to clean up the Mermaid Kingdom. Ready? I wish to clean up the Mermaid Kingdom!

There is still garbage in the kingdom! We're going to need help from our ocean friends!
Say "Clean-up time!"
¡Excelente! Mermaid Kingdom is getting clean.

Now we have to rescue Mariana. *¡Vámonos!*
Let's pull the net off of Mariana. *¡Muy bien!* Now she is free!

¡Mira! The net fell on the octopus, and he has fallen in the garbage.

The octopus promises to put all garbage in the garbage dump from now on, instead of on the Mermaid Kingdom! Hooray! *¡Lo hicimos!* We did it!

Mariana needs her crown back, but she gave me a magical mermaid necklace so I can visit her anytime.

I know that we'll be friends forever, just like you and me! Thanks for helping me save Mariana and the Mermaid Kingdom! I couldn't have done it without you.

DORA saves the SNOW PRINCESS

adapted by Phoebe Beinstein
based on the teleplay by Chris Gifford
illustrated by Dave Aikins

¡Hola! Today I'm reading a book to all my friends. Do you like books? We love books! Boots, Tico, Benny, and Isa really want to hear a story about a snow princess, a witch, and a snow fairy. Do you see a story like that?

Once upon a time there was a little girl named Sabrina who loved snow. Sabrina lived in a lonely, dry forest where it never snowed. One day during a walk, she saw a little white dove sitting in a tree, crying.

"What's wrong?" Sabrina asked the dove.

"I'm caught in a trap set by a mean witch, but no one will free me because they're all afraid of her." The dove showed Sabrina his trapped foot.

"I'll free you!" said Sabrina, and she helped him out of the trap.

"You are very kind and brave," the dove said. "You must be the one! Follow me. I have something special to show you." The white dove led Sabrina to several bushes. "It's behind the bush with the purple berries," said the dove.

Sabrina looked behind the bush and saw something beautiful sticking out of the ground.

"It's a magic crystal!" the dove said. "Now look into it and smile."

So Sabrina did, and the most amazing thing happened.

It started to snow! Then Sabrina became the Snow Princess and the white dove became the Snow Fairy.
"Me, a princess?" Sabrina asked.

"Yes. The forest was under the Witch's spell, but because of your bravery and kindness all the snow animals are free!" said the Snow Fairy.

Everyone in the forest was very happy, until one day the Snow Princess saw the Witch flying in the sky. The Witch suddenly swooped down and grabbed the crystal out of the Snow Princess's hand. She made a mean face into the crystal to stop the snow, and then locked the Snow Princess in the top of a tower.

"Now it will never snow again. Ha! Ha! Ha!" said the Witch before she flew away.

The snow in the forest began to melt. The animals looked for the Snow Princess, but they didn't see her anywhere, so they asked the Snow Fairy to find her. The Snow Fairy knew he didn't have much time before everything melted.

Look! The Snow Fairy is flying right out of the story! He
thinks I'm the Snow Princess!

Hi, Snow Fairy! I'm not the Snow Princess, but I think we
can help you find her because we know where she is—in
the tower! Let's jump into the book and help the Snow Fairy
find her. Are you ready to jump? Jump, jump, jump!

Now we need to find out where the tower is. Who do we ask for help when we don't know which way to go? Yeah, Map! Map says we need to go across the Icy Ocean, past the Snow Hills, and through the cave. Then we'll reach the tower.

I see the Icy Ocean down this big hill. Benny's pulling a sled that we can ride on.

Oh, no. I see that sneaky fox, Swiper. He's going swipe the Snow Fairy! Quick, say "Swiper, no swiping! Swiper, no swiping! Swiper, no swiping!"

Good job! You stopped Swiper.

Here we are at the Icy Ocean, but we need a boat to go across. Look, there's the Pirate Piggies' ship! We love the Pirate Piggies. Will you help us call them? Say "Pirate Piggies!"

They're coming to help us. Let's get on their ship! Watch out for icebergs!

Look! That iceberg isn't an iceberg. It's an icy sea snake coming right towards us! The Witch must have done this. But the Pirate Piggies know just how to scare an icy sea snake. All you have to do is yell "Arrrrrrg!" really loud. Will you be a pirate and help us scare the snake? Ready? Yell "Arrrrrrg!" Wow, what a great pirate you are!

Yay! The Pirate Piggies got us across the ocean and we found a snow hill, but Boots says this snow hill is moving. Wait . . . this isn't a snow hill. Snow Fairy says that the Witch turned the hill into a polar bear! Does the polar bear look happy or angry? Angry? Uh-oh. We'd better run!

There's a girl with a dog sled. Maybe she can help us! Her name is Paj. Paj says she can take us away from the polar bear and right to the cave.

Wow, Paj's dogs run fast! To get around the hills, we have to lean. Will you lean left? Great! Now let's lean to the right. Good leaning! Paj and her dogs helped us get away from the polar bear and brought us to the cave.

This cave is really dark. Do you see a way out? Yeah, up there! Let's climb up and out.

Now we can see the tower and the Snow Princess! But first we have to pull down the drawbridge to get to her. Snow Fairy is trying to fly to the switch, but since he's almost melted, he can barely fly. He might fall in the moat filled with crocodiles! We need to help Snow Fairy fly! Will you help Snow Fairy fly? Flap your wings! Flap, flap, flap! You helped the Snow Fairy! Nice flapping.

Snow Fairy was able to fly all the way to the switch and we reached the Snow Princess. She says the Witch put a spell on her and now she can't smile. If she can't smile into the crystal then it won't snow and everything will melt.

I see the Witch coming now! Maybe I can pretend to be the Snow Princess and smile into the crystal. You can help me smile too.

Now I look just like the Snow Princess! The Witch thinks I'm the princess and that I can't smile, but do we have a surprise for her! We'd better hurry before everything melts. Will you help me smile into the crystal? *¡Uno, dos, tres!* SMILE!

We did it! Our smiles made it snow again, and the Witch lost her powers forever! Now the Magic Snowy Forest is safe!

The Snow Fairy dressed us all like princesses and princes. But anyone can feel like a prince or a princess if they're kind and brave and like to help friends! Thanks for being kind and brave and helping us. *¡Adiós!*

Dora
✦ saves
Crystal
Kingdom

adapted by Molly Reisner
based on the teleplay by Chris Gifford
illustrated by Dave Aikins

¡Hola! I'm Dora. Today I'm reading a special story called *The Crystal Kingdom* to my friend Boots. Do you want to hear it too? Great!

Once upon a time there were four crystals that helped light the Crystal Kingdom. The yellow crystal made the sun shine yellow. The blue one made the sky and ocean blue.

The green one made the grass and trees green. And the red crystal joined the other colors to make a beautiful rainbow! The townspeople loved their colorful world.

But the king did not like sharing the crystals. "Mine, mine, mine!" said the greedy king. He used his magic wand and took all of the crystals for himself. Without the crystals, the town lost all its wonderful color! But the king would not return the crystals. Instead he hid them in other stories where no one could find them!

A brave girl named Allie wanted to rescue the crystals. She searched all over, but they were nowhere to be found.

Look! My crystal necklace is flashing! It's shining a rainbow into the kingdom where Allie lives!

Allie is flying out of her story and into our forest! She needs our help! The Snow Princess says my magic crystal will shine only if there's still color in Allie's kingdom. We have to help Allie find the crystals to keep her home shining! Will you help us too? *¡Fantástico!*

Hmmm . . . how will we find the crystals? Let's ask Map! Say "Map!"

Map says the yellow crystal is in *The Dragon Land Story*, the green one is in *The Butterfly Cave Story*, the blue one is in *The Magic Castle story*, and the red crystal is in *The Crystal Kingdom Story*! We've got to jump into my storybook to get all the crystals! Say *"la primera historia"* to get us into the first story.

¡Muy bien! It worked! There are lots of dragons here. We must be in *The Dragon Land Story*. The Snow Princess has another message for us. She says to find the yellow crystal, we must save a fighting knight. *¡Vámonos!* Let's go!

There's a knight fighting a dragon! But that's a friendly dragon! We need to lasso the sword away from the knight. Backpack has a rope we can use to lasso the sword. Say "lasso" to help me lasso the sword! Good job!

The knight and dragon are happy that they stopped fighting. And the dragon knows where the yellow crystal is hidden! He saw the king put it inside a cliff. *Wheeee!* Let's fly the dragon to the yellow crystal!

Whoosh! The dragon is using his fire to blast open the cliff! We see the yellow crystal! But so does the king! He wants to steal the crystal, but the knight raises her shield and blocks his spell! Yay! We all worked together to get the yellow crystal. And the knight is giving us her shield to help us with the rest of our journey! Thanks, Knight!

Next we need to find the green crystal in *The Butterfly Cave Story.* Say *"la segunda historia"* to get us into the second story.

We're here in *The Butterfly Cave Story*! Uh-oh! My crystal is losing color. That means color is fading from the kingdom. We've got to get that green crystal fast! Do you see the Butterfly Cave? *¡Vámonos!*

There's a caterpillar, and she's stuck! *The Snow Princess* says we can save her by shining sun into the cave. What do we have that's shiny? *¡Sí!* The shield! The sunlight is helping the caterpillar turn into a butterfly. *¡Una mariposa!* Now she can take us to the crystal!

The green crystal is inside the twelfth cocoon. Will you help us count to twelve to find it? One, two, three, four, five, six, seven, eight, nine, ten, eleven, twelve. Great! We found the green crystal. Oooh! The butterflies are hatching from the cocoons. And they're giving us each a pair of magic butterfly wings to help us on our adventure! *¡Muchas gracias!*

Now we've got to find the blue crystal in *The Magic Castle Story*. Say *"la tercera historia"* to get into the third story! *¡Muy bien!*

We made it into *The Magic Castle Story*. There's someone here who can help us! His name is Enrique, and he's a magician.

The king took Enrique's bunnies from his magic hat and put the crystal inside it. Then he locked Enrique out of the castle! We need to find five of Enrique's lost bunnies. Do you see them? Good job!

We used our butterfly wings to fly up through a castle window! To get the crystal out of the magic hat, we have to say "Abracadabra." Say "Abracadabra!" Yay! Allie has the yellow, green, and blue crystals now. Enrique gives us his magic wand to help on our adventure. *¡Gracias, Enrique!*

All we need is the red crystal to save the Crystal Kingdom! To get us into the fourth story, say *"la cuarta historia!"*

We're in Allie's kingdom, but it's still losing color! And so is my necklace! The Snow Princess says that we have to use what we learned to get the red crystal from the king.

The greedy king has the crystal in his crown! What can we use to fly up to him? Right! Our butterfly wings! Whoa! Rocks are coming right at us! What can use to block the rocks? Yeah, the shield!

The king does not want to share his crystals. He's trying to take them from Allie with his magic wand! To break the king's spell with our magic wand, we need to say "share!" Say "share!" Yay! It worked! We got the red crystal!

The color is coming back to Crystal Kingdom! We did it! The king is surprised that we are sharing the crystals. He sees that everyone is happy, and he wants to be happy too. Wow! The king gives Allie his crown and makes her the queen! *¡La reina!*

The town is throwing a party to celebrate the return of the crystals! The king is so happy that he learned how to share. Thanks for helping us save Crystal Kingdom! We couldn't have done it without all our brave friends . . . and especially you.

Dora's Fairy-Tale Adventure

adapted by Christine Ricci
based on the teleplay by Eric Weiner
illustrated by Susan Hall

Once upon a time....

Dora and Boots were playing in Fairy-Tale Land.
Suddenly when Boots wasn't looking, a mean witch cast a spell and turned him into Sleeping Boots! The people of Fairy-Tale Land told Dora that the only thing that could wake Boots was a hug from a true princess.

Dora was worried. She didn't know any true princesses. "I have an idea!" exclaimed a friendly dwarf. "*You* can become a true princess and wake up Sleeping Boots."

The dwarfs told Dora that in order to become a true princess she had to pass four tests. First she had to find the red ring. Then she had to teach the giant rocks to sing. Then she had to turn winter into spring. And finally she had to bring the moon to the Queen and King.

Dora immediately set off to find the red ring. But it was hidden in a dark and scary cave. Dora didn't want to wake the Dragon who lived in the cave, so she quietly tiptoed inside. There she spotted the glow of the red ring.

But just as Dora reached for the ring, the Dragon awoke!

Dora quickly slipped the ring onto her finger. In a flash the Dragon's cave turned into a beautiful palace. And the mean dragon was transformed into a prince!

The Prince told Dora that the Mean Witch had turned him into a dragon. He was so grateful to Dora for setting him free that he gave Dora a magic music box.

"This will help you become a true princess," said the Prince.

Dora thanked him and started down the path toward her next test.

Soon Dora came upon the Giant Rocks.
"How can I teach these Giant Rocks to sing?" she wondered.
Then Dora remembered the magic music box that the Prince
had given her. She carefully turned the handle.

The music box started to play the most wonderful tune. The music was so delightful that Dora was sure it would make anyone sing and dance.

"*Boingy, boingy, boingy, bing. We'll get these rocks to sing!*" sang the magic music box.

Slowly the Giant Rocks opened their eyes. And then, to Dora's amazement, they began to dance and sing!
"*Boingy, boingy, boingy, bing. You've taught us how to sing!*"

When the song was over, Dora told the rocks that she had to be on her way.

"Sleeping Boots needs my help!" she said.

"Wait!" exclaimed the Giant Rocks as they gave Dora a present. "Here's a little bag of sunshine to help you become a true princess."

Dora thanked the Giant Rocks and ran down the path.

Soon Dora started to feel cold. Snow began to fall and a chilly wind whirled all around her.

"I must be in Winter Valley," she thought. "How will I turn winter into spring?"

Suddenly she remembered the little bag of sunshine. Dora opened the bag, and a small sun floated up into the sky.

The sun's rays melted all the snow. Flowers bloomed. Leaves grew on the trees. Birds, butterflies, and animals came out to play in the soft new grass.

"Thanks for turning winter into spring," said the animals.

"Take this magic hairbrush," said a little rabbit. "It will help you become a true princess so you can wake up Sleeping Boots."

At last Dora came upon a castle. She climbed the stairs to the top of a high tower. Now Dora faced the hardest test of all.

"How am I going to bring the moon to the Queen and King?" she wondered.

Dora looked up at the moon and knew that she was going to need some help from her friends.

Isa, Tico, and Benny heard Dora's call for help. But before they could reach her, the Mean Witch made the stairs to the tower disappear. Then Dora had a wonderful idea. She took out the magic hairbrush and began to brush her hair. With each stroke her hair grew longer until it hung all the way down to the ground.

Dora called down to her friends. "Come on! Climb up my hair!"

Dora asked Isa, Tico, and Benny to help her figure out a way to get to the moon. The friends thought hard, and soon they had a plan: They called to the stars!

The stars twinkled and glowed as they flew down from the sky. Then they made a staircase that led all the way to the moon!

Dora climbed and climbed until she reached the moon.

"¡Hola, Dora!" said the moon. "How can I help you?"

"Moon," said Dora, "I need you to visit the Queen and King."

When the moon heard about Sleeping Boots, he agreed to help her and floated down to the tower.

145

"Dora," said the King. "You have found the red ring. You have taught the Giant Rocks to sing. You have turned winter into spring. And you have brought the moon to the Queen and King. You are now a true princess!"

The moon glowed in the sky. The stars twinkled. And rainbows danced through the air as Dora magically turned into a true princess!

"Hooray for Princess Dora!" everyone cheered.

147

The King's unicorns flew Princess Dora all the way back to Sleeping Boots.

Princess Dora wrapped her arms around Sleeping Boots and gave him the biggest hug ever! And then . . . Sleeping Boots opened his eyes!

And so Sleeping Boots awoke at last. The Mean Witch flew far, far away and was never seen again. And everyone in Fairy-Tale Land lived happily ever after!

The End

Dora's Pirate Adventure

adapted by Leslie Valdes
based on the teleplay by Chris Gifford
illustrated by Dave Aikins

Ahoy, mateys! I'm Dora. Do you want to be in our pirate play?
Great! Let's go put on our costumes!

Uh-oh. That sounds like pirates. Do you see pirates? The Pirate Piggies are taking our costume chest! They think it's full of treasure.

If we don't get the costumes back, we can't dress up like pirates. And if we can't dress up like pirates, then we can't put on our pirate play.

We can get our costumes back. We just have to know where to go. Who do we ask for help when we don't know where to go? Map!

Map says the Pirate Piggies took the treasure chest to Treasure Island. We have to sail across the Seven Seas and go under the Singing Bridge, and that's how we'll get to Treasure Island.

Do you see the Seven Seas? Yeah, there they are!
We can use that boat to sail across!

¡Fantástico! Now it's time to sail the Seven Seas. Let's count the Seven Seas together. *Uno, dos, tres, cuatro, cinco, seis, siete.*

Good counting!
Now we need to find the Singing
Bridge. Where is the bridge?

Yeah, there it is. *¡Vámonos!*

The Singing Bridge sings silly songs.

Row, row, row your boat,
Gently down the stream,
Merrily, merrily,
    merrily, merrily,
Life is but a
    bowl of spaghetti!

We have to teach him the right words.
Let's sing the song the right way.

Row, row, row your boat,
Gently down the stream,
Merrily, merrily, merrily, merrily,
Life is but a dream!

163

Yay! We made it past the Singing Bridge! Next up is Treasure Island. Do you see Treasure Island? Yeah, there it is!

Look! There's a waterfall. Isa has to turn the wheel, or we'll go over the edge.

Uh-oh! The wheel broke! Maybe Backpack has something that will help us. Quick, say "Backpack!"

We need something to fix the wheel. Do you see the sticky tape?
Yeah, there it is! *¡Muy bien!*

Turn the wheel, Isa!
Whew! We made it past the waterfall.
Come on! Let's go to Treasure Island, and get our costumes back!

We found Treasure Island. Now let's look for the treasure chest. We can use Diego's spotting scope.

There it is! Come on, mateys, let's go get our costumes back!

The Pirate Piggies say they won't give us back our treasure.
We need your help. When I count to three, you need to say
"Give us back our treasure!" Ready? One, two, three:
Give us back our treasure!

It worked! *¡Muy bien!* The Pirate Piggies say we can have our treasure chest back!

Thanks for helping us get our costumes back. Now we can put on our pirate play. We did it! Hurray!

adapted by Suzanne D. Nimm
based on the teleplay by Valerie Walsh
illustrated by Tom Mangano

¡Hola! I'm Dora! Today is Friendship Day: *¡El Día de la Amistad!* On Friendship Day friends around the world have parties and wear special friendship bracelets. If we wear our bracelets, we'll all be friends forever and ever! Do you want to see the friendship bracelets?

The friendship bracelets are so beautiful!
Oh, no! There's Swiper, and he's trying to swipe our
friendship bracelets! Let's stop Swiper from swiping our
bracelets. Say "Swiper, no swiping!"

Look! Swiper has been swiping bracelets from all around the world. But he didn't know they were special *friendship* bracelets. There won't be a Friendship Day unless everyone has a friendship bracelet, Swiper! We need to return them!

Swiper and I are going to travel around the world and return the bracelets to all our friends for Friendship Day. Will you come with us? Great!

Who do we ask for help when we don't know which way to go? Yeah, Map!

Map says that to return the friendship bracelets to our friends, we have to go to the Eiffel Tower in France, to Mount Kilimanjaro in Tanzania, to the Winter Palace in Russia, and to the Great Wall of China.

¡Vámonos! Let's go around the world!

We're in France! And this is my friend Amelie! To say "hello" to Amelie in French, we say "*bonjour*." Let's say "*bonjour*" to Amelie. *Bonjour,* Amelie!

Amelie is going to help us bring the bracelets back to the Eiffel Tower.

Amelie says that the smiling gargoyle will help us find the Eiffel Tower. There's the smiling gargoyle! The smiling gargoyle says that we need to follow the street with the diamond stones. Do you see the diamond stones? Great! We'll go that way!

Yay! Swiper is giving everyone at the Eiffel Tower their friendship bracelets! Oh, no! Fifi the skunk is sneaking up on Swiper. Fifi will try to swipe the bracelets. Help me stop Fifi! Say "Fifi, no swiping!"

Hooray! We stopped Fifi! Now all our friends
in France have friendship bracelets.
There are many more bracelets to return.
¡Vámonos! Let's go!

We made it to Tanzania. This is my friend N'Dari. To say "hello" to N'Dari, we say "*jambo*." N'Dari says that everyone is waiting for the friendship bracelets at Mount Kilimanjaro.

Quick, we have to take a safari ride to the mountain! Along the way we have to watch out for wild animals. How many zebras, lions, giraffes, hippos, and elephants do you see?

Hmm! I think I hear another wild animal. It sounds like a hyena. Do you see a hyena? That's Sami the hyena! He's going to try to swipe the bracelets. Will you help me stop Sami? Say "Sami, no swiping!"

Yay! We stopped Sami! Come on, everyone! Come and get your friendship bracelets!

Now we have to bring the friendship bracelets to the Winter Palace in Russia. Do you see something that can fly us there? The hot-air balloon! Great idea!

189

We made it to Russia! But the Troll won't let us inside
the Winter Palace.

My friend Vladimir can help us. Vladimir says the Troll will open the gate if we make him laugh. Let's make silly faces to get the Troll to laugh! Make a silly face!

What great silly faces!

Our silly faces made the Troll laugh, and he opened the gate! And look! The Winter Palace is filled with lots of friends! Let's say "hello" to everyone. In Russian we say "*preevyet!*"

The children decorated the Winter Palace for Friendship Day! There are icicles, balloons, flags, snowmen, and even a dancing bear!

Fom-kah the bear is very sneaky. He's going to try to swipe the friendship bracelets. Help us stop Fom-kah. Say "Fom-kah, no swiping!"

Yay! We stopped Fom-kah! Now we can return the friendship bracelets to our friends in Russia.

We have more bracelets to return. *¡Vámonos!*

We made it to the Great Wall of China. Wow! What a party! But we have to make sure these bracelets stay safe. Watch out for Ying Ying the weasel. If you see him, say "Ying Ying, no swiping!'

This is my friend Mei. To say "hello" to Mei, we say "*knee-how*." Mei is helping us give out the friendship bracelets.

Hooray! We returned all the friendship bracelets. Now we can start the Friendship Day celebration!

We made it back home for our Friendship Day celebration. We have eight friendship bracelets left. How many friends are at our party? *¡Siete!* Seven! They all get a friendship bracelet.

And there's one more bracelet! It's a friendship
bracelet for you—because you're such a great friend!

197

Wow! The bracelets are glowing! Rainbow sparkles are lighting the sky all over the world! Thanks for helping us save Friendship Day! Now we'll all be friends forever and ever! We did it!

At the Carnival

adapted by Leslie Valdes
based on the teleplay "The Big Piñata"
illustrated by Robert Roper

Hi, I'm Dora. Do you like to play games? Me too! Boots and I
are at a carnival. That's a festival where you play games and
win prizes! Boots and I want to win the grand prize—the Big
Piñata!

When a piñata breaks open, all kinds of prizes fall out—like toys and stickers and treats!

To win the Big Piñata we need to collect eight yellow tickets.
Will *you* help us win the Big Piñata? Great!

How do we get to the Big Piñata? Let's ask Map. Say "Map!"

"Hurry, hurry, hurry!" calls Map. "You have to go past the Ferris wheel, then go around the merry-go-round, and that's how you'll get to the Big Piñata."

Along the way we'll collect the eight yellow tickets by going on rides and playing games.

We made it to the Ferris wheel! Look—it's Señor Tucán! He says we can ride the Ferris wheel, but first we have to find an empty seat.

Will you help us find an empty seat on the Ferris wheel? What blue shape is next to it?

Yay! You found the empty seat next to the blue star! Señor Tucán says we won four yellow tickets!
Now we can ride the Ferris wheel. Higher and higher and higher we go! Whee!

Next we'll go to the merry-go-round! Do you see it?

Here's Isa the iguana. Isa says that if we ride the merry-go-round and find the orange ring, we can win more yellow tickets.

Will you help us find the orange ring?
¡Excelente! You found it!

We just won four yellow tickets! Yay!
Let's see. We had four yellow tickets from before, and now we just won four more yellow tickets.

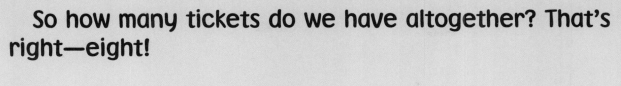

So how many tickets do we have altogether? That's right—eight!

215

Now we can win the Big Piñata! Do you see it? Come on, we're almost there!

Uh-oh, that sounds like Swiper the fox! That sneaky fox will try to swipe our tickets!

Do you see Swiper? We have to say "Swiper, no swiping!"

Thanks for helping us stop Swiper. We made it to the Big Piñata!

"Step right up!" says the Fiesta Trio. "You need eight tickets to win."

We have eight tickets. *¡Fantástico!* We won the Big Piñata!

Look! All of our friends are here to help open the Big Piñata.

To open the Big Piñata we need to pull the green ribbon. Do you see the green ribbon? Reach out and grab it with both hands. Pull!

Hooray! We opened the Big Piñata! And look—there are toys and stickers and treats everywhere. Thanks for helping! *¡Adiós!*

The Birthday Dance Party

Daisy's Fiesta de Quinceañera

adapted by Alison Inches
based on the teleplay "Daisy, La Quinceañera"
by Valerie Walsh
illustrated by Dave Aikins

¡*Hola!* I'm Dora, and this is Boots. Today we're going to my cousin Daisy's fifteenth birthday party—her *fiesta de quinceañera.* That's a special birthday party where she'll become all grown up!

Boots and I need your help to deliver Daisy's present—her special crown and shoes—to wear at her party. She can't start the party without them!

Will you help us take the crown and shoes to Daisy's *fiesta de quinceañera?*
Great!

Map says we have to go past the Barn and then through the Rainforest to get to Daisy's party!

Remember to watch out for that sneaky fox, Swiper. He may try to swipe Daisy's present. If you see him, say "Swiper, no swiping!" *¡Vámonos!* Let's go!

There's the Barn! Hey—do you see that funny-looking duck?

Wait—that's not a duck! It's Swiper the fox!

Oh, no! Swiper swiped Daisy's present and threw it on that conveyor belt. It's rolling away! We have to get Daisy's present back.

If the present is on the conveyor belt with a circle flap, say "*¡Círculo!*" If the present is on the conveyor belt with a triangle flap, say "*¡Triángulo!*"

Quick! Which conveyor belt is the present on?

¡Círculo! ¡Sí!

We got Daisy's present back *and* we made it past the Barn.
Thanks for helping! Now we need to go through the Rainforest.
But look! There's a rain cloud over the Rainforest. We can't let
Daisy's present get wet!

Do you see something in my Backpack that can keep us dry in the Rainforest?

¡Sí! ¡El paraguas! The umbrella! That can keep us dry. Good thinking!

We made it through the Rainforest without getting wet! And there's my cousin Diego with Baby Jaguar. Diego is Daisy's brother.

¡Hola, primo!

Diego is on his way to Daisy's *fiesta de quinceañera* too.

We can go together! Come on!

Ding! Dong! Ding! Dong!
The bells are ringing! It's time for Daisy's party. But the party can't start without us because we have Daisy's crown and shoes!

We need to hurry! Diego says the giant condor birds can fly us to the party quickly.

Look—there's the party! And there's my cousin Daisy. Happy birthday, Daisy! We have your special crown and shoes, so you can start *la fiesta de quinceañera*!

But first Boots and I need to put on our fancy party clothes too!

Now it's time for the ceremony to begin. Daisy's *mami* is crowning her with the special crown we brought to her. Daisy's *papi* is helping her into her grown-up shoes. Wow, Daisy really *does* look all grown up!

Now it's time for Daisy and her *papi* to walk arm in arm down the aisle. Let's clap and cheer for Daisy!

Now it's time for dancing! Let's all do the mambo dance.
I love to mambo! Do you want to mambo with us?

Here's how you do it:
   First march in place . . .
   then wiggle your hips . . .
   now wave your hands in the air!
You're doing the mambo!

Mambo! Mambo! We did it! Thanks for helping us get to Daisy's party. We couldn't have done it without you!